Magical Mayhem

Part Six

To Prevent Cute Mascots

Emily Martha Sorensen

Also by Emily Martha Sorensen

Standalones:
Black Magic Academy

Fairy Senses:
Fairy Eyeglasses
Fairy Compass
Fairy Earmuffs
Fairy Barometer
Fairy Pox
Fairy Slippers
Fairy Lunchbox
Fairy Icepack
Fairy Stopwatch
Fairy Toothbrush
Fairy Perfume

Dragon Eggs:
Dragon's Egg
Dragon's Hope
Dragon's First Christmas
Dragon's Fire

Comics:
A Magical Roommate
To Prevent World Peace

Picture Books:
Tabby, Tabby, Burning Bright

The End in the Beginning:
The Keeper and the Rulership
The Fires of the Rulership
The Magic or the Rulership

Trilogy of a Teenage Werevulture:
Trials of a Teenage Werevulture
Trifles of a Teenage Werevulture

The Numbers Just Keep
Getting Bigger:
Twenty-Four Potential
Children of Prophecy

Not Quite a Harem:
Not Quite a Curse

Magical Mayhem:
To Prevent World Peace
To Prevent Chic Costumes
To Prevent Clear Paths
To Prevent Smart Choices
To Prevent Warm Welcomes

Short Story Collections:
Worlds of Wonder

To Prevent Cute Mascots

To Frederik Vendelin,

longtime fan of the comic,
reader of my other books,
and Patreon supporter.

Chapter 1
The Nuisance

Zigzagging around the piles of half-finished machine clutter, a ten-year-old leapt for Kendra's wrist and grabbed it.

"Are you going on a mission? Can I go with you this time? Please please please please?! Please please please please?! Please please please please?!"

"*No!*" Kendra shouted, wrenching her wrist away. The pesterer had done this every day for the past week. She was starting to feel homicidal. "And let go of me!"

Tiffany went rolling backwards, but she held up her left hand with a hideous atrocity of feathers in it.

"But you *have* to!" the nuisance wailed. "I've got a costume and everything!"

Kendra tried. She really did. But she couldn't quite suppress a shudder of horror at the ten-year-old's apparent "costume."

It wasn't the lilac shorts with cutesy lace underneath. It wasn't the matching sandals, which would absolutely fly off at a moment's notice in the middle of a battle. It wasn't the powder blue sleeveless blouse with the little pink hearts on it. It wasn't even the crimson cape that was safety-pinned lopsidedly to the girl's shoulders, giving the clear impression that this was a magical girl costume, not a villain's.

No, it was the atrocity held in the girl's hand, which was meant to be perched upon her face.

"First of all, that mask is *not* a costume," Kendra said in utter disgust. "It's an abomination of hot pink glitter, mismatching fake jewels, rhinestones, and feathers."

"It's pretty!" Tiffany declared.

"You have no taste whatsoever. Second, you're a nuisance, not a teammate."

"Am so!"

"Third," Kendra said, "I bet the teleporting watch can't even take two people —"

"Actually, it should," Chronos interrupted from the corner. She was sitting in a plush armchair and crocheting something out of a small ball of yarn. "The original power worked that way."

Kendra was taken aback for a moment. "Original . . .?"

"Sure. My uncle's born mage power was to steal magical abilities," Chronos said, not looking up from her crocheting. She wasn't terribly good at it; she went slowly, and she kept on making mistakes that resulted in garbled patterns and knotted yarn. "He did that, and he sealed them into objects. Doing that killed the person who'd had the magic, so he mostly only did that with enemies. Great-Uncle Nico routinely had him harvest the born mage power of anyone in our family who was on their deathbed, though."

Kendra shivered. Now that she'd found out about the oracle being an Olympian, Chronos was hiding nothing else about it. Kendra wasn't sure if she was trying to drive her away from villainy by purposefully bringing up the ugliest things, or whether the woman simply thought such things were normal. She always spoke about stuff like this in a flat voice, as if she had no opinion about any of the awful things her relatives had casually done.

"For instance, he killed some teleporting magical girl to make that thing," Chronos said flatly.

Kendra gaped at the teleporting watch strapped around her wrist. She'd assumed it was some sort of technology brought from another world, perhaps one of the high-tech mascot worlds.

Somebody had *died* to make that thing?

The Nuisance

A magical girl had *died?*

Kendra scrambled to unbuckle the watch and held it over her head, staring at it. It seemed so innocent: a clunky, old-fashioned digital watch that anybody with terrible taste in fashion might wear. It didn't seem like something a person had *died* to create.

But she should have realized something was off. Teleportation was a very rare power. Teleportation that could reach anywhere across the world, and didn't even require you to have been to that place before, was even rarer. She should have realized that if a watch like this could simply be bought, a few magical girls and a lot more villains would have one.

Kendra cursed herself silently for having missed such an obvious conclusion. Why had she even been thinking it had come from a high-tech mascot world in the first place, anyway? The most high-tech mascot world she knew of had machines made of crystals that were powered by rainbows, and this watch was nothing like that. It was clearly Earth technology.

For that matter, why had she jumped to mascot worlds instead of minion worlds in the first place? Chronos was a villain. Chronos was an *Olympian.* The chances of her having ever met a mascot were extremely remote. It wasn't like mascots allying with villains was unheard of, but it was very uncommon.

Mascots usually didn't have much that a villain might want. A lot of this had to do with the fact that there were two kinds of magic systems across the many worlds.

One kind of magic had its source inside the person using it. Born mages were the ones native to Earth, though there were more from other worlds. If you had this kind of magic, you had it; if you didn't, you never would.

The other kind of magic had its source inside the planet. Some magic systems like that could be used by everybody; others, like the magical girl magic system, could only be used by those who met specific requirements. Magic like this could be gained or lost.

It also *didn't work outside its own world.*

Which was why most mascots had nothing to offer villains, but they did have something to offer magical girls.

Born mages could wander between worlds with impunity. So could their equivalents from other worlds. Because they were their own source of magic, they couldn't leave it behind, no matter what they did. If you opened a portal and offered them magic that they could only use in a world they didn't live in, they'd shrug and be unimpressed.

The first magical girl to make a deal with a mascot — most likely sometime in the late 1910s, though nobody knew precisely — had probably assumed that everything would go as expected. She'd use her magical girl powers on Earth, she'd dabble in the magic of the mascot's world whenever she visited, and being able to visit another world and play with a new type of magic there would be more than payment enough for helping solve whatever crisis they had come begging for help with.

It hadn't turned out that way.

Because it turned out that there wasn't just *one* characteristic of the magical girl magic system that made it unique.

There were *two*.

The first was, of course, the obvious fact of transforming. No other magic systems out there seemed to require people to transform to use them. Even more crucially, no other magic systems created a second life with which a person could literally die, and yet still stay alive in their original unmagical form.

Kendra's mom had written an entire book about the two unique traits of the magical girl magic system, and she had spent more than seven-eighths of it discussing transformation and just how special it was, and how bizarre it seemed to people from other worlds. The second characteristic had been little more than an afterthought tucked in the back. But while it was only of passing interest to most magical girl scholars, it was of critical importance to people from other worlds.

Magical girl power could hybridize with other magic systems.

This meant that, yes, born mages could become magical girls, and in fact there used to be a lot of born mage magical girls in the early days of the magic system, which some politicians liked to insist proved that not all born mages were evil, yada yada yada.

But far more importantly, it meant that if a mascot brought something to a magical girl that tied in to a planet-based magic system of their own world, she could accept it and then use *both* magic systems within *both* worlds.

Born mage magical girls? They could travel to other worlds and use both magic systems.

The equivalent of born mages from other worlds? They could open up a portal, send their daughters to Earth for five minutes, have them gain magical girl powers, and then fetch those little girls back to their home world, where they could use those magical girl powers until they outgrew them. Which was why people from humanoid worlds rarely asked for help from magical girls — they could easily make their own.

Not that it was legal to do that without express permission from an Earth government, but it was pretty hard to stop them.

Meanwhile, mascots couldn't do that. Only humanoids or humans could become magical girls. If a mascot shapeshifted into a humanoid while on Earth — in other words, if they had a born mage-like power to shapeshift that would travel to another world with them — they'd be capable of gaining magical girl powers while humanoid, which they could then take back to their own world. But otherwise . . . nope.

So mascots very often wanted help from magical girls. And they very often had something valuable to offer that the magical girl couldn't get in any other way. Plus, a lot of them tended to be cute, which helped a lot when it came to persuading little girls to want to spend time with them.

Kendra had never had a mascot, but she'd always been open to the idea of working with one.

Maybe if she had found one to work with, she would never have had to worry about Avenging Angel, would never have had to give up her magic, would never have had to become a villain . . .

"If you don't want that watch anymore, I'll take it!" Tiffany exclaimed excitedly. "I'll travel around and fight bad magical girls in your place! I'll name him Warren. No wait, Wiley. No, wait, Willy. No, wait, Wally!"

Kendra jumped. She realized she'd been standing there, staring at the watch, for several minutes. Hastily, she shoved it in her right jeans pocket. "NO WAY!"

Chronos was eyeing her speculatively.

"Oh, I know what you're thinking," Kendra said darkly.

Chronos sighed heavily and rolled her eyes.

"You're thinking, 'Using a thing implies consent.' But I don't subscribe to that philosophy. Just because it was wrong to make something doesn't mean it shouldn't be used after it's made."

"Amazingly, that wasn't what I was thinking."

"And I know you're thinking, 'But somebody died to make it!' But if more lives can be saved with it than without, then it would be wrong not to use it. Sometimes the ends really do justify the means, oracle. You might think that that sounds extreme, but it's true."

"Astonishing," Chronos said dryly. "How did you know I was thinking that? Are you a mind reader?"

"Just very perceptive." Kendra shrugged.

"You're flat-out *wrong!* I was being sarcastic!"

Kendra folded her arms, deeply annoyed. "Fine. Then why were you staring at me?"

Chronos looked exasperated. "If you must know, I was thinking that if you took Tiffany with you, I'd get peace and quiet for once."

"Yes!" Tiffany cried excitedly. "I'll be the best teammate ever!"

"You're not a teammate!" Kendra yelled.

"Anyway, I think you ought to take Tiffany." Chronos unwound a bunch of yarn from off the ball on her lap so that she could keep crocheting. "A little time outside the lair would probably be healthy."

"Absolutely not!" Kendra declared. "And you can't make me!"

"Really?" Chronos asked tartly. "Because I *could* stop telling you which targets to chase."

Kendra turned away, squeezing her shoulders tightly. It was an impossible situation. The soothsayer might very well do that, and then Kendra would have to resort to eavesdropping on her during her sleep again. It was very inconvenient to do that. Chronos mostly only mumbled about generalities, not specific times or places, which made it very hard to count on those for intel.

The Nuisance

Not that this stopped Kendra from sitting there eavesdropping after any day Chronos had given her nothing to act on, mind you. Kendra got antsy if she wasn't keeping busy, and sometimes she got tips to ask about the next day. Chronos threw a fit whenever Kendra asked for details about a specific dream she'd mumbled about the night before, ranting about privacy or something, but that was really not a very interesting subject to Kendra, so she tended to tune those lectures out.

Kendra didn't want to take Tiffany with her. She really, really didn't want to take Tiffany. But she also didn't want the oracle to stop giving her intel. Of course she could wear Chronos down eventually, but the days that would pass during which Kendra would have nothing useful to do would drive her crazy.

". . . Fine . . ." Kendra muttered, barely audibly.

The other two immediately started planning behind her back.

"Now, dangerous mission or more subtle variety?"

"Dangerous!" Tiffany yelled. "No, wait — more subtle variety!"

Kendra spun around to watch them chattering as if this were an exciting occasion, rather than a disastrous idea. "Am I the only one who sees a problem with dragging a ten-year-old into a combat situation?!" she burst out.

Chronos gave her a flat look. "Kendra. You fight ten-year-olds every day."

"Only competent ones!"

Chronos ignored her and turned back to Tiffany. "Now, here's an interesting person I've been meaning to send Kendra after . . ."

Above her arm hovered the image of a magical girl and an egg-shaped critter with a long tail and catlike ears.

"A mascot!" Tiffany squealed. "It's so cute! Can I hug it?"

Kendra's face smacked her arm as her head fell and her arm rose up to meet it. "We are going to fail miserably."

Tiffany shoved her mask on her face and posed.

"The Cute Avenger is all ready!"

Chapter 2
The Answer

Nearing an electric pole with a flier on it, Florence's mood did not improve to see that it held a picture of her best friend.

Kendra stood there in her new black outfit, holding her spiked halo threateningly. She looked menacing and villainish, not even possibly-redeemable-because-she's-trying-too-hard-so-she-must-be-brainwashed, like a dark magical girl would.

Florence hated that wanted poster. She hated it. It made her best friend's terribly stupid decision seem irreversible. Those things were all over town, even on the walls of the school, and whenever she saw one of them, she wanted to scream and tear it down.

Is she really past the point of no return now? Florence wondered, staring at it.

Originally, Kendra had done little to attract the interest of the police. She'd gone around proclaiming herself a villain, and she'd fought magical girls and sometimes killed them, but she'd never harmed a human life, and her targets had been so sporadic that nobody had been able to find a connection to predict them. Since the police had had much better things to worry about, they hadn't tried much.

All that had changed with Blue Donkey and Red Elephant. After that disaster, Kendra had caught the FBI's attention.

And now she was on the Top Ten Most Wanted Villains list. And there were wanted posters everywhere.

Why? Florence raged. *Why, why, why, why did you feel the need to show up at a major political rally and break the focus items of both of the magical girls performing there? What was the purpose? Why would you do something so pointless that was bound to enrage so many people?*

The police had been kind enough to not publicly reveal Kendra's secret identity, but that hadn't really helped much. Everyone all over town had noticed that Kendra was missing, and "Seraph" didn't wear a mask in those blasted posters. It had taken everybody in town less than one second to draw the obvious conclusion.

"Is that what happened to Kendra? Did she get brainwashed by a villain? Hey, come to think of it, she kind of looks like that Cream Angel magical girl who used to run around town, doesn't she? Does that mean you were Pink Dragon?"

After the eighth busybody had straight-out asked her about her secret identity, Florence had flatly replied, "Do you think all black people look alike?" That had shut them right up.

But snideness wasn't a long-term solution. There *was* no long-term solution to her secret identity being blown.

Everyone had guessed Felicity's secret identity, too, and at first, she'd hesitantly admitted it. But when the reaction had consisted of a whole lot of attention, almost all of it positive, she'd eagerly started volunteering stories about her amazing time as a magical girl. She'd now been interviewed on TV three times.

Florence had been invited to be interviewed, too. She'd refused all of the invitations, a lot of them not very politely.

And as bad the whole thing was for her, Florence felt even worse for Kendra's mother. Her career was in shambles over her daughter now being a wanted criminal. The magical girl community had been shocked and horrified at the scandal of a well-known writer of magical girl biographies having a daughter who'd defected to villainy. As if Kendra's mother had had anything to do with that in any way! Kendra's father seemed to be doing okay, but he rarely showed much emotion, anyway.

Florence's mom had been spending a lot of with Kendra's mom recently. According to her, when people went through the worst thing they could possibly imagine, they needed lots of extra care and attention.

Which made sense, and Florence got that, and she totally agreed . . .

. . . but nobody was doing that for her.

Her best friend was the cause of all her problems, so it wasn't like she was around to help, and Florence didn't make friends easily, so she didn't have a lot of other people she could pour her heart out to.

There were her parents, but . . . Florence was fifteen. She wanted to feel like she could figure things out herself.

Felicity had an entirely new social group, including a best friend and a boyfriend, and she was enjoying her new celebrity status.

In fact, in her cynical moments, Florence wondered whether Daniel had agreed to be Felicity's boyfriend entirely because of it. It seemed pretty suspicious to Florence that he'd completely ignored her until the day after Felicity had gotten her first TV interview, and then he'd immediately started telling everyone she was his girlfriend.

Felicity had been overjoyed.

Florence had been disgusted.

That had been ten days ago.

It's been almost six months since Kendra quit, Florence thought gloomily. *Two weeks since Felicity. Twelve days since the wanted posters went up . . . but who's counting?*

She forced herself to walk away from the wanted poster. But the brooding thoughts followed her.

I joined because of Kendra. I've never been a magical girl without a team. Until now. Now I'm alone . . .

When she was twelve, she'd thought fluffy pink dresses and magenta-and-gold tiny bat wings were the best things ever. Now, she hated her magical girl form. She hated everything to do with it. She hadn't transformed since the day Felicity had quit and left her standing behind, all on her own.

She could quit, of course . . . but she hated that idea, too. She wasn't Felicity, throwing away something precious just because she couldn't see the value of it right now.

But maybe . . . maybe she was just clinging to something because she was too scared to let go. Maybe she *ought* to quit? The more she thought about that, the more confused she felt. She reached home with her mind in turmoil.

Her dad was on the living room couch, totally absorbed in reading a Bible and taking notes. He was probably preparing for next Sunday's sermon.

Florence hesitated for a moment, and then she spoke up.

"Dad? Is it irresponsible of me to be considering quitting?"

Her father blinked and shook himself. He looked back at her, then laid the Bible on his lap. "Quitting what? The track team?"

"No," Florence said, plopping her elbows on the top of the back of the couch. She leaned her chin onto them. "The whole 'magical girl' thing."

"Oh." Her father was silent for a moment. "Well, I guess that depends on your reasons."

Florence climbed over the back of the couch and flopped onto the seat beside him. Their mother was forever telling her and Jacob not to climb on the furniture that way, but her father made no comment.

There continued to be silence. Her father waited, his finger flicking at the corner of the Bible page as if he really wanted to go back to it, but he didn't want to show it. Florence pretended not to notice, because she didn't want to be polite and let him go back to work. She really wanted advice.

"Everyone else in my team quit," Florence burst out. "I feel like, what's the point of being a magical girl without them?"

"Mm." Her father nodded.

"I mean, I know magical girls are supposed to be able to help save the world and all," Florence said uncomfortably. "And I know we've done some good things. But I just . . . don't want to do that anymore. I never really wanted to go around stopping crimes with violence in the first place."

"Mm-hm." Her father nodded.

"I did it because of Kendra," Florence complained. "She really wanted to be a fighting magical girl, and I really wanted to be a magical girl with her, so I was willing to fight. But now she's gone. Even Felicity is. And everyone's guessed my secret identity, which means the secret, the last little bit of fun left, is gone from it!"

"There are plenty of magical girls without secret identities," her father said. "Snowbelle in Antarctica, for instance —"

"*I* wanted a secret identity!" Florence exclaimed.

Her father shut his mouth and nodded. "Mm-hm."

"So what am I supposed to do now?" Florence added. "I could be a singing magical girl, I guess, but that seems so boring. Singing magical girls don't do anything important."

"I think the four posters of Lentswe Counterpoint in your room would beg to disagree," her father said dryly.

Florence waved her hand. "She's an anti-apartheid activist. All her concerts are basically political rallies put to music. But I mean, that's kind of my point! She's not *just* a singing magical girl. She is one, but she's far more than that. She's a symbol of an entire movement. If I became a singing magical girl, what would I do? Be a flash-in-the-pan singer with maybe one hit, if I was really lucky? That's not exciting! That doesn't have any meaning!"

"So you're looking for meaning," her father said.

"Yes!"

"Well, what would have meaning for you?"

Florence started to answer, then stopped. "Now you ask the *hard* questions. Thanks."

Her father laughed. "You might say that's my entire job."

That was the problem with her dad. He never gave her answers. He just gave her more questions. It was seriously annoying sometimes.

"I *should* stay a magical girl in order to save the world, right?" Florence hedged. "That's what magical girls do, right? As long as I have power, I have responsibility, right? Giving it up would be irresponsible, right?"

Her father's eyebrows raised in amusement. "You're not trying to convince me to guilt-trip you into staying, are you?"

"I . . ." Florence hesitated. "I don't know!"

Her father laughed.

Florence glared down at her knees. "It's just that, on the one hand, I want to do something meaningful. On the other hand, I'm not sure just how meaningful my magic actually *is*."

"You can do good in the world without magic," her father said. "Look at Gandhi."

"Gandhi had magical girls on his side!"

"Yes, who he forbade to use magic to solve any problems. Every time they tried, he went on another hunger strike."

Florence sighed. "Okay, fine, Dad. Just tell me what you think I should do."

Her father reached out and embraced her with one arm. "You need to make your own decisions, Florence."

"But I feel dissatisfied about leaving," she moaned, hunching her shoulders. "I feel stagnant about staying. What does that leave?!"

Her father was silent.

"Dad," Florence pleaded, "please don't do the thing where you don't give me any advice at all, and you just give me a whole bunch of questions instead. I'm really confused right now."

Her father spoke slowly. "Questions are all I've got, Florence. I can't tell you how to live your life, or what you want to do with it."

"But I need answers!" she exclaimed.

Her father drew a deep breath, and let it out. "Well, obviously I'm going to tell you to pray. But beyond that . . . when people are confused, that usually means they're asking the wrong questions. Correct answers don't help if the questions are wrong. So perhaps you're asking yourself the wrong questions. If you figure out the right one, everything else often falls into place."

"Then what would the right question be?" Florence asked.

He set the Bible aside and hugged her with both arms. "I have no clue, I'm afraid. That's up to you. But once you know, your mother and I will support you with whatever you need."

It was an answer, not a question. But perhaps it was a beginning.

Chapter 3
The Mascot

Even if she'd been forced to take a dreadfully horrible ally with her, Kendra was determined to make this mission a success. Three people were about to die if she failed, after all.

"Now, you heard everything about the magical girl," Kendra said, checking one last time with Tiffany before they teleported. "You heard about her powers."

"Yep. They're greasy lightning."

"*Greased* Lightning. Her name is *Greased* Lightning."

"Uh huh, she zaps people with greasy lightning."

Kendra was not feeling confident about her so-called teammate's preparation for this mission so far.

"What about the mascot?" she prompted.

"He looks cuddly and his tail is heart-shaped at the bottom and he's adorable."

"*And?*" Kendra snapped.

"And I wanna squish him because he looks squishy."

"*AND?!*"

"Kendra, you do realize that the darklings have already appeared and are fighting Greased Lightning right now, don't you?" Chronos asked from her armchair. She was trying to untangle a huge mess of tangles she had made with the yarn.

Kendra jumped. "Hurry up! Take off that mask! Hold my hand!"

"Maisie stays on!" Tiffany said stubbornly.

"Approximately fifteen seconds before one of them dies," Chronos announced.

"MASK!"

"NO!"

"Twelve seconds."

There was no time to quibble. Kendra grabbed Tiffany's hand and teleported them both to the place where Greased Lightning, her mascot, and the darklings were supposed to be. For a second, she was disoriented, hearing sounds of a battle and not seeing one. Then she realized that she'd teleported them to the wrong side of the house.

Tiffany must have realized a split second before she did, because she was already racing around the corner.

"Remember their powers!" Kendra yelled, breaking into a run herself. "— And take off that stupid mask!"

"NOOOOOOOOOOOO!" Tiffany yelled.

They rounded the corner just in time to see the back of a magical girl with a long whip whirling it around her head and generating terrifying arcs of lightning.

"*Rumbling Flash!*" the magical girl cried.

Three gigantic lightning bolts lanced out and shot towards the three darklings. The egg-shaped creatures with pointed ears and fangs and diamond-shaped tails fell to the ground and lay still.

Dead? Kendra thought frantically. *Are we too late?*

But no — two were still breathing. Hopefully all three were.

"Oh, thank you, Greased Lightning!" a squeaky, sycophantic voice cried. "You've saved us from the evil darklings once again!"

Kendra spun around to look at Greased Lightning's mascot. He was an egg-shaped fuzzy creature with rounded ears, a heart at the end of his tail, and gigantic, watery eyes. He looked like a floating stuffed animal, and he sounded like a character from a children's show.

He wasn't.

"Light Seed Collection!"

The mascot opened his mouth wide, almost taking up his entire egg-shaped body. There were four prominent sharp teeth on the top and on the bottom, exactly like with the darklings, except these had been hidden. A swirling vortex appeared in the back of his throat, and a purple diamond at the bottom of each of the darklings' tails glowed.

The air around the vortex trembled, and the diamonds burst off the darklings' tails and zoomed towards the mascot. Kendra had only a split second to react.

She flung her halo at the mascot, and it knocked the thing off balance. He went flying, the vortex vanished, and the diamonds went tumbling.

Greased Lightning spun around and saw her for the first time.

The halo zoomed back at Kendra, and she caught it perfectly, her fingers curled around the four-inch spot with no spikes.

Nailed it! Kendra felt a swift surge of pride.

She was holding it now in the exact same place she had been holding it at the time it had grown spikes, so that section was exactly the right size for her grip. But it had still taken a lot of practice before she'd learned to grab the spinning, bladed halo out of the air without cutting herself.

"Yeah. Don't feed your mascot. It's a bad idea," she said.

The magical girl gaped at her, apparently unable to form a coherent sentence.

"Greased Lightning! Villain!" the mascot squeaked from the place on the ground where he had thudded down a few seconds earlier.

The magical girl shook herself and started to spin her whip around her head. "Chaaaaaaaaaaaaaaaaaarge —"

According to Chronos, Greased Lightning had to charge her ultimate power for several seconds every time she wanted to use it. It was a major design flaw that Kendra would have sneered at if she hadn't been facing it.

Since Kendra was facing it, she didn't stop to sneer, and merely flung her halo out and smacked the spinning whip out of the girl's hand.

"HEY!" the magical girl cried.

Kendra lashed her hand into the air and caught the halo as it spun back to her again. This time, her aim was ever-so-slightly off, and her pinky nicked the edge of a spike, but she ignored that.

"Tiffany!" she yelled, having seen with her peripheral vision that her not-a-teammate had raced over to them. "How are the darklings?"

"They're not cute!" the little girl reported.

"Are they alive?!" Kendra shouted.

"I think so!"

The egg-shaped fuzzball with the heart-shaped tail drifted up into the air. He started to open his mouth —

"NO!" Kendra yelled. She flung the halo at him again, and he went flying.

Greased Lightning dashed for the diamond-shaped purple things that had scattered across the grass. Kendra flipped through the air and kicked her away. The magical girl spun around and kicked at her head, just slowly enough that Kendra easily dodged.

"You're helping that thing under false pretenses!" Kendra informed the girl. "It's not the victim you think it is!"

"Cupid is a hero!" the Australian magical girl yelled back. "He has to save his planet from the evil darklings!"

Kendra ducked an elbow the girl smashed at her face, then whipped her halo around to slice the magical girl across the chest. But Greased Lightning had already jumped back and was bolting towards her whip.

Oh, no, you don't! Kendra thought.

Kendra flung her halo out into a wide arc. A blurry ring of blades swished across Greased Lightning's path, causing her to yelp and jump back. Kendra was already running forward, and the enemy's split-second hesitation was enough for her to catch up. She grabbed the girl by the back of her red midriff-baring blouse and threw her down to the ground.

"Your so-called 'Cupid' isn't even a different species from the darklings!" Kendra yelled, catching the halo as it spun back to her hand. "Are you really so stupid that you failed to notice how similar they look? They even use the same technology to survive!"

The magical girl rolled to the side, avoiding Kendra's boot as she tried to stomp it down to break the girl's wrist.

"They *are* different species!" the girl yelled in her Aussie accent. "The darklings are invaders from another world!"

"Not even close!" Kendra shouted.

"Light Seed Collection!" a squeaky voice called from behind the two of them.

"ARGH!" Kendra shouted in rage, and flung her halo back at the floating mascot, just in time to stop the diamonds from zooming into his mouth again. "Tiffany, you idiot, would you do something?!"

"That's not very nice!" the little girl protested. "And call me the Cute Avenger!"

Kendra spared no more time for her stupid not-a-teammate. Greased Lighting was already back on her feet, and had already seized her whip.

"Charge —"

"Light Seed —"

"TIFFANY!" Kendra screamed, diving for the magical girl and knocking her off her feet. This time, Greased Lightning managed to hang on to her whip.

"Hey!" a squeaky voice cried. "Greased Lightniiiiiiiiing!"

Kendra's head whipped around to see Tiffany lifting up the mascot by both of its weak little arms and holding it up to her face. The legless creature lashed its tail and shrieked in terror.

"Ooh! Is this the evil thingy?" she asked in delight, bouncing the thing up and down in the air to watch it wriggle. "It's so cute! The darklings aren't cute at all!"

"Helllllllp!" the mascot howled.

"Cupid! Let go of my mascot!" Greased Lightning hollered, slashing her whip out to its full length. The tip didn't quite reach the little girl's face.

Tiffany didn't even blink from behind the hideous mask, looking profoundly unimpressed. "And lose my hostage? No way."

"CHARGE LIGHTNING!" Greased Lightning screamed.

Kendra cursed silently. That was exactly what she'd been trying to stop the magical girl from saying.

The whip started to crackle, almost ready to unleash into its ultimate attack. Kendra gave up on stopping that, and bolted for the diamond shapes in the grass instead.

"No! The light seeds!" the mascot exclaimed.

"*Rumbling Flash!*" the magical girl shouted, unleashing her ultimate attack upon Kendra.

Kendra teleported off to the side. The lightning hurled harmlessly past her and blasted into a tree, leaving a black spot in the middle. Then Kendra teleported next to the diamond shapes so that she could grab them and protect them. She hated using the watch in combat, since it was ugly and she didn't want to rely on it, but time seemed of the essence right now.

"I'm going to name you Squishyfuzzy," Tiffany informed the mascot, swinging it back and forth by its dangling arms. Whether it was by accident or on purpose, this served to keep the thing from biting her, despite its efforts.

"That's not his name! His name is Cupid!" Greased Lightning shouted, momentarily distracted.

Kendra considered using that opening to fling her halo again, but this might also be a chance to talk some sense into the girl.

"Oh, ignore her," she said, picking up one of the diamond shapes. It made her fingers tingle, pulsating with an odd electrical power. "We're not after you, anyway. Has it ever occurred to you to wonder why your mascot wants these power sources so badly?"

"To save his planet from the evil darklings!" the magical girl snapped, raising her whip.

Stupid, stupid credulous kid.

". . . Not hardly," Kendra snorted. "Your lovely little friend here is an eco-terrorist in his world. And darklings are the *police*."

Chronos had shown them a plethora of the mascot's futures. One of them had had the creature bragging to a bunch of other critters who looked like the darklings about how he'd gotten the magical equivalent of plastic surgery to make himself look cute so that a magical girl would trust him. The other critters had then flown off to get themselves modified the same way and to find more gullible magical girls to use the same way.

This was not a future Kendra found desirable.

She had, in fact, been outraged. Abusing the trust of innocent magical girls in order to manipulate them into using their magic for evil was *not* okay.

The magical girl looked uncertain. Her eyes flicked to the squirming mascot. Her eyes flicked to Kendra, who was busily pocketing the diamond-shaped things.

As soon as the mascot swallowed those things, they'd be converted into whatever kind of magical energy he used to fuel his weapons back home, but as long as the diamonds stayed away from him, they'd continue to function for their intended purpose, which was generating life support for the three unconscious darklings.

Apparently the reason that particular species had never come to Earth before was that they breathed a different type of air, and the technology to overcome that was a new innovation.

A new innovation that the mascot had stolen, naturally. The heart-shaped thing on its tail was a life support generator, too.

The magical girl's eyes flicked uncertainly over at her mascot. "Charge Lightning?"

Kendra grinned. That would be fitting.

"Don't listen to the villain, Greased Lightning!" the egglike creature squealed from Tiffany's grasp.

"I'm not!" the magical girl shouted. *"Rumbling Flash!"*

The whip was faster than Kendra, who had not expected it to go in her direction. It lashed around her body, twisting around and binding her. Lightning arced, and Kendra blacked out.

As she came back to herself, fuzzily, she felt the magical girl pick up her limp body and say disdainfully, "I trust my mascot much more than I trust *you.*"

Kendra was flung to the ground. She couldn't seem to move.

"Now let go of my mascot!" she heard the girl yell. "Charge Lightning — Rumbling —" There was a pause. "— Huh?"

Kendra lifted her head. The mascot was lying on the ground in a heap, looking as dazed as she felt. Tiffany, who Kendra had wrongly trusted to keep guarding the mascot and stop it from attacking the unconscious darklings, was nowhere to be found.

The Mascot

Where did that brat go? Kendra wondered in irritation.

She gritted her teeth and clenched her fist, relieved that she seemed to be able to move again. Carefully, Kendra brought her arm holding the halo forward —

"Don't worry, Kendra! I'll save you!" the nuisance shouted.

Kendra's head shot up, and she saw the little girl running towards her, mask flying off as she raced straight towards Kendra, exactly the opposite direction that would have been helpful.

Greased Lightning spun around. She lifted the whip above her head and spun it to charge her lightning, no doubt to attack the two of them at once.

Before she could speak the words, Kendra flung the halo to smack the girl with the flat side across the back.

Greased Lightning sprawled forward. The whip went flying.

Kendra snatched her halo as it whooshed back to her hand. She was still lying on the ground, but she wasn't incompetent.

"I don't need saving," she growled to Tiffany.

Tiffany stopped, looking devastated.

Kendra leapt to her feet, dusting herself off furiously and trying to ignore the pain that ached its way all over her body.

The magical girl was lying on the ground in a heap. She was breathing heavily, but seemed to be still. Perhaps she'd knocked herself unconscious. Well, that would make everything easy.

A fuzzy, sharp-toothed creature suddenly flung itself at her, scrambling for the diamond-shaped things in her pocket.

Kendra seized the mascot by the tail and held it at an arm's length, spinning it around rapidly so that it couldn't escape the centrifugal force and attack her.

"L— L— L—!" the thing kept shouting, trying to activate the thing that let it eat the life support diamonds, but that didn't seem to be working. It didn't seem to be able to even get out the first word. Which was good, because Kendra didn't really want to kill the mascot, but she would if she had to. She took a dim view on people corrupting magical girls.

Tiffany's head drooped. Her lips formed a pout. "Well, I *almost* helped . . ."

"You didn't help at all," Kendra snapped. "You got in the way. *Helping* would have been distracting Greased Lightning by going in the opposite direction, not running right towards me where she could attack us simultaneously!"

"But I wanted to help!" Tiffany cried.

"Do you even know what 'help' is?!"

"G-G-Greased Lightni-i-ing!" the mascot howled as Kendra spun him. Her arm was starting to get tired, but she ignored that. She was good at ignoring pain when she needed to. "A-a-attack Kendra!"

What? Kendra thought for a split second. *How does he know my name?* And then she realized Tiffany had yelled it while running towards her. That was the last straw.

"Seraph!" she yelled, looking at Tiffany. She spun the mascot even harder in her rage. The thing howled. "While we're in a battle, call me Seraph!"

"But you didn't call me the Cute Avenger!"

"You didn't tell me to! I told you to call me Seraph!"

"I did so tell you!"

"No, you didn't!"

"Did so!"

"Didn't!"

"Did so!"

"Didn't!"

"I'm going to tell Chronos you're being unfair!"

"Tell her whatever you want, but don't talk about people who aren't here on the battlefield! Are you stupid? Why would you tell our enemies things you don't have to?" Kendra yelled.

At this point, Kendra's right arm was killing her, so she flung her halo out in front of her, tossed the mascot by the tail, caught its tail in her other hand, and resumed spinning it with her left arm, which was less sore. Then she caught the halo in her right hand as it arced back, jabbing her thumb against one of the spikes.

"You're so mean!" Tiffany yelled. "Kendra, Kendra, Kendra, Kendra, Kendra!"

"I'm not mean — I'm right! And for the last time, call me *Seraph!*"

Tiffany posed dramatically. "Okay, then you have to call me . . . the Cute Avenger!"

". . . Pass."

"That's not faiiiiiiiiir!"

Ignoring her, Kendra walked over to check out the darklings, still spinning the mascot to keep it from attacking her. The three darklings were still lying still, but they were breathing. Either their life support was weaker because they didn't have those diamonds with them, or Greased Lightning's attack was more potent on those creatures than it was on humans. It wouldn't be a surprise if that was the case, since they were only a sixth the size of a human.

Tiffany wandered over and followed her. "What do we do with these thingies?" she asked, picking up one of the darklings by the tail and holding it, dangling.

"We give them back their life support systems," Kendra said, elbowing her pocket with her right hand that was full of halo. "Get 'em out and put 'em back on their tails, would you?"

"Yay! I'm helpful!" Tiffany beamed, dumping the darkling back on the ground and hopping over to Kendra. She tugged the three diamond shapes out of the pocket and hopped eagerly back to the darklings, where she poked the things back onto their tails. "They're not as ugly now!"

"Yay," Kendra said, rolling her eyes.

"What are we gonna do with the evil thingy?" Tiffany added, looking at the mascot in Kendra's grip.

Kendra slowed down the speed at which she was spinning it as she thought about that. Her left arm was getting tired, anyway. "We find out if Australia has an extradition treaty with their world, or even better, their specific country. If so, we drop him off at the Interworld Consulate. If not, we'll have to wait until the darklings wake up and see if they can portal him back —"

There was a sudden jerk, and the mascot broke free of her loosening grip. It darted away before she could grab it successfully. As soon as it was fifteen feet away from them, it opened its mouth and started: "Light Seed —"

Kendra teleported to the mascot, snatched it by the tail, and shook it really hard up and down. "BAD CRIMINAL!" she shouted.

"Waah!!" the thing yowled.

"Oh, there's my mask!" Tiffany cried. She ran over to where it had dropped, which was near the fallen magical girl, and grabbed it. Unfortunately, she immediately put it back on her face.

There was a murmur from the fallen figure. "Rumbling . . ."

Kendra leapt to the side.

". . . *FLASH!!*"

The whip lanced through the air and wrapped itself around Tiffany.

"*Ow ow ow ow ow ow ow ow* —"

The mascot swung towards Kendra's elbow, sharp teeth exposed. She snatched its head and stretched the thing until it looked like *The Scream*.

"*Wrong,*" she told it.

The magical girl was turning towards her —

KONG! Kendra swung the mascot around and whapped her upside the head with it.

The handle of the whip went flying out of her hands, and the end of it wrapped around Tiffany loosened.

With tears in her eyes, the nuisance summoned her wand and waved it around until sparkles came out of it. "BREAK IT!"

The whip instantly shredded and exploded every which way.

Kendra stared at Tiffany, stunned.

What —? Wait. Did she just —?

Could Tiffany's BREAK IT power actually break magical girl focus items?!

It wasn't like Kendra couldn't do that. But her halo had to hit one exactly right, magical girls were really good at protecting their focus items, and Tiffany's power was *ranged*. It didn't even need to be aimed!

Maybe, just maybe, Kendra thought, her mind spinning, *the Cute Avenger might be a good teammate, after all.*

"Ow . . . Guh?!"

Then Kendra heard somebody screaming.

She glanced over and saw Greased Lightning's transformation dissolving all around her. Her midriff-baring red blouse and short pleated skirt sparkled into a plain sundress. Her spiky bangs and side ponytail glimmered into a short, messy ponytail on top of her head. Around her, sparks and ash were blowing into the wind —

The now-human magical girl screamed even louder.

Kendra snorted, making her halo disappear and grabbing the mascot's tail at the base with her other hand. Holding it upside down in that position kept its mouth from being able to reach her to bite. "Somehow, I don't feel too sympathetic. If you'd listened to me, or you'd been a little less gullible in the first place, this wouldn't have happened."

Come to think of it, holding the mascot still with both hands was a lot easier. She should have done that in the first place.

"Take that, you horrible meanie!" Tiffany shouted, pointing an accusing finger at the now-human Greased Lightning. "That's what you get for hurting the Cute Avenger! Your magical girl form is dead now! You'll never transform again!"

Kendra was really tempted to let that inaccurate comment stand, but the magical girl had only been stupid. The girl presumably hadn't intended to kill a bunch of police officers and shield an eco-terrorist, even though that was what she had been doing for weeks. Stupid as she was, Greased Lightning didn't deserve to think that she'd have no second chance to make things right.

"What we said about your mascot was true," she said bluntly. "Go to the Australian Mascot Bureau and ask. If he'd been legitimate, he would have gone through proper channels."

The girl scrambled away backwards, her face a mask of sheer terror, as Kendra walked towards her.

Losing your magical girl form in front of a villain had to be frightening. Kendra got that. She'd been powerless in front of villains before. But she'd seen other magical girls deal with it much better than this. A girl she'd fought in Melbourne last week had nearly defeated Kendra *after* losing her magical girl form. And as Cream Angel, Kendra had never been so wimpy.

The mascot wriggled and tried to shout, "Light Seed —"

Kendra spun and smashed its furry face down on the ground until it seemed to be unconscious. Stupid thing wasn't going to get the hint unless she beat that into it, it seemed.

The now-human Greased Lightning whimpered.

I'm not gonna kill your human life, Kendra thought in exasperation. *Villains who do that are scum. And if you think I'm about to do that, why don't you fight back?*

"Now," Kendra said sharply, "because you're apparently too dim to figure this out, Tiff— the Cute Avenger broke your focus item. She didn't kill your magical girl form, so you're still a magical girl. You're still capable of transforming. You just need to make a new focus item before you can access your magical girl form again. You'll be able to do that in twenty-four hours, and it will last as long as you don't go near the villains who broke your other one — if you go near us with the new one, it'll break automatically."

Those last two parts were a complete lie. One particularly annoying battle Kendra had been through had featured a magical girl who had created a new focus item approximately two seconds after Kendra had broken her old one five times in a row, resulting in a really long and exhausting battle that had only ended when Kendra had just killed the girl's magical girl form.

Seeing as Kendra was not an idiot, she figured she might as well make sure this girl didn't realize she could create a new focus item and decide to start attacking again right now. Creating a new focus item wasn't easy — it required a lot of will and concentration, so it took most magical girls days or weeks to do it — but there was no reason to take the risk.

"We win!" Tiffany said triumphantly, picking up two of the darklings, one in each hand. The things were still unconscious. "What do we do next?"

"Take them to the Interworld Consulate?" Kendra shrugged. She scooped up the third darkling and held it in one hand as she dangled the now-former mascot over her shoulder. "I assume they have a way to contact other worlds to ask them to open portals so that they can send illegal aliens and unwanted criminals back to their own worlds."

"Or we can open a portal ourselves!" Tiffany said excitedly. "We could visit another world!"

"Gee," Kendra snorted. "Why didn't I think of that? Going to another world with a poisonous atmosphere to humans would be a great idea. Other than the fact that it's almost impossible to open a portal from a higher-magic world into a lower-magic world, and our world has the highest level of magic in the vicinity . . ."

Since both of her hands were full, Kendra reached out to put her elbow on top of Tiffany's head, so that she could teleport the kid and also the four otherworlders.

"Oh, I know!" Tiffany burst out. "Let's ask the darklings to send *us* a mascot!"

Kendra stared at her incredulously. "We're villains. They're the police for their people. Are you insane?"

Chapter 4
The Question

Beginnings weren't endings, and Florence was starting to get really sick of not knowing what question she ought to be asking herself. Not to mention that school had taken a nosedive to become even more unbearable than it had been before.

It wasn't so much the wanted posters in the hallways. Having twenty-seven (she'd counted) all over the school seemed excessive, but she was used to those by now. It wasn't so much the students staring at her and whispering, or the popular girl loudly mocking Pink Dragon's choice of fashion whenever Florence walked by her, or the two hate notes that had been tucked into her locker blaming her for not stopping Kendra from becoming a villain.

Those hate notes had been shoved into her locker the day after Kendra had killed the magical girl form of a popular magical girl actress who had starred in a sitcom that was popular with girls in their school. Naturally, nobody had any clue why she'd done that, including Florence.

Anyway, it wasn't any of those things that were the problem. Florence didn't like being mocked, but it was pretty easy to ignore the same predictable snide comment, she knew perfectly well that Kendra's defecting wasn't her fault, and as for people pointing and whispering . . . that was going down gradually on its own.

The Question

Nobody had an unlimited attention span for the same rumor that never changed, after all. A lot of other rumors had started to grow over the ones about Florence and her former teammates, including one that said Felicity's boyfriend was cheating on her and she was absolutely clueless.

That particular rumor made Florence want to throw things, especially because it was probably true. She was pretty sure she'd seen him at a movie with a girl who wasn't Felicity. She had even tried to tell her former teammate, because friends or even former friends should do that sort of thing, but Felicity had just waved her hand and ignored it.

This was one of the two reasons school had gotten unbearable. Having been through an evil boyfriend who'd used her and then discarded her, Florence couldn't stand to see a friend make the same mistake. But there was nothing she could do about the awful situation if Felicity wouldn't listen. Felicity had even started to avoid her after she'd brought up the subject the first time.

Okay, so Daniel probably wasn't a villain out to literally kill them all, like Lute Deathwave had been. He was probably just a cad who enjoyed the attention of his supposed girlfriend being on TV and so forth. But it was still frustrating, and Florence hated to see it going on without being able to fix it.

The other thing that made school unbearable was the fact that Kendra's mother had gotten permission from the principal to start an after-school "brainwashing defense class" that she taught for free to any students who wanted to show up. Since Kendra was in the news a lot, a lot of curious people kept going.

Florence had overheard Kendra's mother telling another parent after one of those classes that she felt it was the least she could do, to make sure no other parents wound up in the position she and her husband were in. The other parent had nodded sympathetically.

And that was . . . fine. It really was. Florence understood why Kendra's mom teaching those classes was a good thing. It might help a few other students, and if nothing else, it gave Kendra's mom something to do other than sitting around watching her career fall apart and her daughter continue down the path of villainy.

The problem was that every time she saw Kendra's mother, it made her feel sick to her stomach. It reminded her of just how empty she felt without her best friend, and then she felt guilty because Kendra's parents had it so much worse, and then she wanted to scream at Kendra for doing this to all three of them, and then that turned into a thought spiral of feeling guilty and angry and miserable, over and over and over again.

Florence really wanted to quit school and go somewhere else. Anywhere else. Somewhere away from all of this. But it wasn't like she could ask her family to move. This was their home. Her parents and brother were all happy here. Three people being happy trumped one person being unhappy. She didn't want to act like a selfish jerk.

Just wait till college, Florence kept telling herself. *You can leave when you go to college.*

Except college was two and a half years away. She didn't have the grades to get into a school years early. She wasn't particularly excited about college, either. It just sounded like more of the same routine of homework, testing, and grades.

Without Kendra trying to shove her down the wrong path, Florence had no idea what she didn't want, which made it hard to figure out what she did.

Track was just about the only thing she still enjoyed going to. And even that had had a few . . . bumps lately.

"People, our track meet last week was *humiliating!*" their coach shouted, pounding her fist into her hand. She was a short-haired woman with a jaw like a rock, and she had been in a bad mood for every practice for weeks. "Miss Jones! If you'd warmed up properly like you're supposed to, you wouldn't have twisted that ankle! Miss Atweil! Yelling at the other team's coach was unacceptable! Miss Khatri! What were you doing at the start?! Daydreaming?!"

Florence stretched her quads along with the rest of the team, and tried to ignore the coach's venting. She didn't show up at practice to hear more people being unhappy. She showed up because she loved running, and it was the one time she felt like all the problems in her life melted away. Running was the one time when she had a clear head, when she felt certain about anything.

The Question

"At least Miss Atkins did decently!" the coach shouted, pacing.

Florence winced as some of the other girls glared at her. Why was the coach singling her out? She wasn't here to compete. She just wanted to run. Couldn't they just have fun? Wasn't that what track ought to be?

The coach moved on to bellowing about their new goals, demanding that they reach a minimum time today or risk being cut from the team.

School these days is so depressing, Florence thought with a sigh.

She wondered what the schools at Mágico were like. She'd heard they had boarding schools for magical girls, and you could go to them for free room and board, as long as you served on the country's defense grid to protect the tiny country from Brazil, their hostile next door neighbor.

Do I want to go there? Florence wondered.

Like many other questions she'd come up with over the past few weeks, it was mildly interesting, but it didn't make her heart zing with the feeling "I have found it!"

The right question. That's what I need, she thought, scrunching her face in concentration. *The right question . . .*

Going to another school, in and of itself, seemed appealing. Leaving her family behind didn't. Heading to an entirely different continent seemed a little radical, especially since most of those schools were in Portuguese.

It would break things out of the status quo, she pondered. *That would help, wouldn't it? Getting out of here without making my family leave would solve most of my problems.*

It would, but maybe . . . maybe it wouldn't, actually. Part of her dissatisfaction came from her magical girl powers, and the fact that she didn't know what she wanted to do with them. Truthfully, she wasn't even entirely sure that being a magical girl would do as much good as she'd always believed. Strongly as she disagreed with Kendra's choice to go into villainy, some of her best friend's words had stuck in her head.

"It's possible for magical girls to turn corrupt. One with sufficient charisma and arrogance could even lead the world to destruction."

That suggested that Kendra believed there was a worldwide problem with the magic system. If Kendra believed that, of all people, it must have taken real evidence to convince her. A problem that was that widespread needed a real solution, not just a band-aid like some ridiculous I'll-be-a-villain-now thing.

Warm-ups finished, Florence wandered over to the starting line with three of her track teammates.

So how do you fix a systemic problem permanently?

Her mouth went dry. Chills ran down her spine. Her heart pounded wildly.

It was the question.

That was the question.

That was the exact question she'd been waiting for.

"WAKE UP, Miss Atkins!" their coach's voice exploded.

Oh! Florence realized, looking up. She had completely missed the starting whistle. Everyone else had already reached the end of the hundred-yard sprint.

She fumbled an apology and ran to the end, but her head was buzzing, and she barely even noticed the rest of track practice as it flew by.

She had her question. Now she just needed to answer it.

At two o'clock in the morning, Florence leapt out of bed. She'd been unable to sleep, her mind humming too much and sprinting across random pathways.

She thought she had her solution, and she needed to talk to somebody else about it. Right now.

She opened her door and ran down the hallway to her parents' bedroom. She swallowed before knocking, aware that she was being really inconsiderate, but she needed to talk to somebody, right now, and there was nobody else to talk to.

"Hello?" her father's surprised voice said.

Florence turned the doorknob and pushed the door open. Her mother was fast asleep with a pillow over her head to block the dim light of her father's reading lamp.

Her dad was sitting up, lit by the dim glow of a reading lamp beside him. He had a Bible in one hand and a highlighter in the other. It was clear he had been thinking too much to sleep, too.

Florence hesitated. Maybe she should just talk to her dad. He was awake right now, after all.

No. She needed her mom, too. Her mom would actually make suggestions, rather than trying to make her figure stuff out on her own, and she needed a second opinion.

"Mom? Dad?" Florence asked softly. "Can we talk?"

Florence's mother groaned and lifted the pillow from off her head. She reached over and groggily pulled a pocketwatch off her bedside table to look at it. "It's . . . two am . . ."

"Sure," her dad said, looking puzzled.

"D'ya need us both?" Florence's mom mumbled. She moved the pillow back on top of her head.

"Yes," Florence said anxiously. She paced across the room, back and forth, and then sat down in the chair by their dresser, her knee jittering up and down as she spoke. "I need you both."

Florence's mother groaned, but she removed the pillow and sat up, looking bleary. "Mmkay. Whass goin' on?"

Florence swallowed, and swallowed again. Now that it had come down to it, she was afraid to start speaking. Afraid that they would tell her she was crazy. Afraid that the idea she'd had was impossible, as impossible as it sounded, and totally ridiculous.

Her mother's eyes started to drift shut.

"I've come to a decision," Florence blurted out. "A decision about what I should do."

Her mother's eyes opened. She rubbed them and nodded, looking more alert.

"About your magic?" Florence's father asked.

"Not just that." Florence took a deep breath. "About everything. About magic itself. I realized Kendra's right that there's a problem with the way people perceive our magic system."

Florence's mother looked very alert now, and downright alarmed. "Florence —"

"Is that . . . right?" her father asked cautiously.

"I'm not going to turn villain or anything stupid like that," Florence said hastily, realizing she'd just freaked her parents out. "I'm not a lunatic."

Florence's mother breathed out a heavy sigh of relief.

Her father's shoulders, which had tensed, now relaxed.

"It's just that . . . I've realized that a lot of people think magical girls are incorruptible," Florence said. "They're not."

"Of course not," Florence's mother said. "To think they are would be to make them an idol."

"Kendra's mom believes they are," Florence said.

"She does not," Florence's mother said immediately. "Olivia has more good sense than that. Magical girls are children, and children are both precious and immature."

"Well . . ." Florence said, not wanting to argue the point, "well, Kendra thinks she believes they are. Kendra believed they were. I think there are a lot of people out there who do."

"There might be some," Florence's father said.

"There might be *lots*," Florence said. "Look at the laws in this country. It's completely legal for magical girls to kill people! There's not even any paperwork to fill out!"

"Fighting magical girls do have to register —" her mom began.

"Registering is not the same as regulating!" Florence exclaimed. "Magical girls have far too much power, and not nearly enough rules they have to follow. People just assume the magic system is self-regulating, but it isn't! It isn't *enough!*"

Florence's mother looked baffled.

Florence's father frowned. "So . . .?"

They didn't understand. Of course not. She still had to explain.

"So Kendra was right," Florence said. "There's a problem, and it needs to be fixed. But she's also wrong. You can't change the law by becoming a criminal."

It was funny that she'd thought she needed a second opinion. Now that she'd said the words out loud, she didn't. She was sure of what she needed to do. It was the future she wanted, and the future she was going to fight to get.

And she knew just how she needed to start it.

The Question

Florence summoned her magical girl bracelet, her focus item, the source of all her power. It roared onto her wrist with a wreath of flame. Without hesitating, she removed it.

She placed it on top of her parents' dresser, along with a jumble of other things.

She would not be Pink Dragon any longer.

"Mom, Dad . . . I want to create a government for magical girls."

www.ingramcontent.com/pod-product-compliance
Lightning Source LLC
Chambersburg PA
CBHW022044050726
47591CB00003B/939